Lily and the Wizard Wackoo

Written by Judy Fitzpatrick
Illustrated by Don Hatcher

An easy-to-read SOLO for beginning readers

SOLOS

Southwood Books Limited
3-5 Islington High Street
London N1 9LQ

First published in Australia by Omnibus Books 2000

Published in the UK under licence from
Omnibus Books by
Southwood Books Limited, 2003

This edition produced for The Book People Ltd.,
Hall Wood Avenue, Haydock, St Helens WA11 9UL

Cover design by Lyn Mitchell

ISBN 1 903207 85 1

Printed in China

A CIP catalogue record for this book is available
from the British Library

For the boys of Wyvern House – J.F.

For the magical little Matilda – D.H.

Chapter 1

On the edge of a lake, in a place far away, there was once a cold, old stone castle. In it lived a king, a queen, and their three lovely daughters.

Princess Lucy could sing like an angel.

Princess Emily played the flute sweetly.

And Princess Lily made magic.

Everyone loved Lucy's singing and Emily's flute playing.

No one liked Lily's magic.

Her spells made flippers instead of slippers.

Her spells made snakes instead of cakes.

Lily's magic made her sisters very cross.

"You are a little FLEA!" shouted Emily.

"Can't you ever make magic that doesn't go wrong?" cried Lucy.

"You need a wizard to teach you," said the king.

"*What* a good idea," said the queen, picking bits of ham out of the jam tart Lily had just made.

At that exact moment, the doors of the castle flew open. In the doorway stood a very old wizard.

Chapter 2

"I want your daughters to make music at my birthday party," the wizard said to the king. "I'm inviting some friends to my cave. My name is Wizard Wackoo."

"Wack what?" asked the king.

"Not Wackwhat," said the wizard. "It's Wack ... Oh dear, now you've made me forget my name."

"You said it was Wackoo," Lily told him.

"Who are you?" asked the wizard crossly.

"She is a little flea who needs magic lessons," shouted Emily.

"Yes, why don't you take *her*," cried Lucy.

"I don't want her, I want *you*," replied the wizard. He pointed a bony finger at Lucy and Emily.

"How will they get to your party?" asked Lily.

"By dragon taxi, of course," said the wizard. "I have one waiting outside. He can travel faster than the speed of light, or sound, or something. I forget what."

"What's the dragon's name?" Lily asked.

"Let me think." Wizard Wackoo scratched his head. "It starts with a D. It's Dennis. No, no. It's Duncan."

Outside the window, Lily could see the dragon. He was puffing out his name in big smoky letters over his head.

Chapter 3

"It's Douglas," said Lily. "You are taking my sisters away on a dragon named Douglas."

"Lily!" shouted her sisters. "Be quiet! We don't want to make music at his smelly old party."

The wizard boiled with rage. "Smelly old party? How dare you!" His face went purple, and he shouted:

"Oh whistling wind
That whirls and swirls,
Roll up tight these unkind girls!"

A whirlwind whizzed through the room. Before anyone could say "Stop!", it had picked up Lucy and Emily. It dropped them on the back of the dragon taxi.

The wizard smiled.

"Hooray! Hooroo! That spell will do!
I still remember a thing or two!"

He turned to the king and queen. "I'll bring back your daughters when my party's over," he said.

"When will that be?" cried the queen.

"Oh, in about a hundred years," replied the wizard.

He jumped onto the dragon taxi
and it shot into the sky like a comet.

Chapter 4

The king and the queen were very upset.

"How will we get our daughters back?" cried the king.

"Where have they gone?" sobbed the queen.

Lily stared at the far-off mountains. Tiny puffs of grey smoke were rising above them. If she half closed her eyes, she could read the words made by the smoke:

Dial Douglas the Dragon Taxi 0000.

"So *that's* where they are," Lily said to herself.

No sooner had she dialled 0000 than Douglas appeared.

"I know what you want," he said. "The wiz won't like it. But I'll take you there, and I'll take you home again. That is, if you ever get out of his cave. Wackoo may be old and forgetful, but he still makes powerful magic."

"You haven't seen *my* magic," said Lily, as she hopped aboard.

Chapter 5

Douglas dropped Lily off right outside the wizard's cave.

"I'll wait here," he said. "Be careful!"

Lily crept into the dark cave. As she tiptoed along, bats flew about her head. The smell of something rotten floated past her nose.

"I must serve a wonderful meal for my birthday," she heard the wizard saying. "I hope I have this recipe right. I mustn't forget the owls' eyes. Or is it eagles' eyes?"

Lily stepped forward boldly.

"Where are my sisters?" she asked. "I have come to rescue them."

The wizard laughed. "They are not here, little flea," he said. "They are at Magic Hill, far away. So how do you think you can rescue them?"

"I don't know," said Lily. "I have trouble remembering my spells. I suppose a great wizard like you never forgets his spells."

"Never," said the wizard proudly.

"I suppose you can even remember a spell to bring my sisters back here and set them free," Lily said.

"Of course I can," said the wizard. "It goes like this:

"Wind, be calm, wind, be still,
Bring those girls from Magic Hill.
Unwind, unwrap and set them free,
Lucy and her sister Emily."

Chapter 6

In a second Lucy and Emily had landed in front of them. They looked very confused.

"Well done!" Lily said to the wizard. "You're very good at this, aren't you?"

The wizard fluffed up his whiskers. "You could say that," he replied.

"I've heard about a spell to make a wizard into a fairy," said Lily. "Do you know that one too?"

"That's easy," said Wizard Wackoo.

"Give me glitter, give me wings,
Give me shiny silver things.
Make me shrink until I'm small,
Until I'm hardly here at all."

As he began to shrink, he glared at Lily.

"You tricked me!" he screamed. "And I can't remember the spell to turn myself back into a wizard!"

Chapter 7

Lucy and Emily rushed over to hug Lily.

"You *are* a clever little flea," they said.

Lily looked down at the tiny fairy. It was jumping up and down and squeaking loudly.

"I'll take you home with us if you promise to teach me all the magic you know," she said.

The fairy nodded. "I promise," it squeaked.

"I might even learn how to turn you back into a wizard," said Lily. "Until then, you must be a very good fairy."

In no time Douglas had taken them back to the castle. The king and queen were very happy to see them.

"I have promised that Wizard Wackoo can stay with us if he teaches me magic," Lily told them.

"That's nice," said the king. "I like a wizard to be useful."

"I can be useful too," Douglas said. "I can take you all shopping. And I can warm up this cold castle with just one puff of my hot breath."

"*What* a good idea," said the queen.

And everyone lived happily ever after.

Judy Fitzpatrick

As a small child I liked reading, singing and being in plays. There were six children in my family. We used to put on our own plays in the back yard and ask other children to come and watch us. We made up stories about wizards and witches, kings and queens and magic. I think that is how I learned to use my imagination.

I enjoyed writing this story because, like Lily, I was the youngest of three sisters. Older sisters often see the youngest as a bit of a pest, but sometimes she can be very helpful – just as Lily was.

Don Hatcher

When I started to do the drawings for this book I thought about how good it would be to be a wizard. I could say a magic spell and always have sharp pencils. I would never get ink all over my fingers. And my bicycle would whizz up steep hills all by itself!

I'm sure, though, that I would forget the spells, as Wizard Wackoo does. Or I might be like Lily. I'd turn my pencils into lentils, my ink would stink, and my bicycle might become an icicle.

No, I think I'd better keep doing scratchy drawings and leave magic to the wizards!

More Solos!

Duck Down
Janeen Brian and Michael Johnson

The Monster Fish
Colin Theale and Craig Smith

The Sea Dog
Penny Matthews and Andrew Mclean

Elephant's Lunch
Kate Darling and Mitch Kane

Hot Stuff
Margaret Clark and Tom Jellett

Spike
Phil Cummings and David Cox

Lily and the Wiazrd Wackoo
Judy Fitzpatrick and Don Hatcher

Sticky Stuff
Kate Walker and Craig Smith